Grandma's Christmas Tree

Written by

Grandma Janet Mary™

Illustrated by

Craig Pennington

2nd Book in the Grandma Janet Mary™ Series

My Grandma and Me *Publishers*

To Grandma Cherie,
I hope this book creates
many Christmas memories
Love,
Craig Pennington
2004

To: Grandma Cherie
May Christmas joy
fill your heart
everyday of the
year.
with love,
Grandma Janet Mary
2004

Acknowledgements

Special thanks to:
Michelle Koenigsknecht for sharing her time and heart as editor of this story.
Allison Ackerly for her special contribution.
Owen Pennington for his very special contribution to this book.
Colleen Koenigsknecht for her helping hands and giving heart are always there.

Grandma Janet Mary™
My Grandma and Me *Publishers*
P.O. Box 144
St. Johns, Michigan 48879
Phone 989-224-4078
Fax: 989-224-3749
Web Site: www.mygrandmaandme.com
E-Mail: info@mygrandmaandme.com

First Edition
Printed and bound in Canada
Friesens of Altona, Manitoba

Library of Congress Cataloging-in-Publication Data on File

ISBN 0-9742732-1-X
LCCN 2004093217

Author's dedication
to . . .

. . . my father and mother, Nick and Marge
and my sisters and brothers,
Ron, Sue, Gary, Karen, Nick, Mary, and Connie
for fun-filled memories
of Christmas past.

. . . my husband, Mike,
and my children,
Jason and Nicole, Emmy and Kevin, Jake and Barb, Sarah and Mike, and Michael and Kim
for loving memories created now
in Christmas present.

. . . my grandchildren,
Ellen Marie, Maddie Mae, Ethan Jacob, Gavin Randall, Murray Michael
and all grandchildren to come,
for joyous memories, yet to be realized
in Christmas future.

- *Grandma Janet Mary*™

Illustrator's dedication
to . . .

. . . my loving wife, Natalie
and my sons, Owen and Guy, whose faces on Christmas morning,
filled with wonder and excitement,
create new and lasting memories that rekindle the magic of the season.

. . . my big brother, Bob, my little brother, Jas
and to my parents, Jim and Kathie, who somehow always kept the peace on
Christmas mornings.

. . . my grandparents, Harry and Irene,
my Aunt Lynn and all members of my family who made
Christmas as a child so meaningful.

- Craig Pennington

To grandchildren of all ages,

There is a kind of magic
in your Grandma's Christmas Tree.
Pine branches like embracing arms
that hold and set you free.

A magic seen in ornaments,
once made by those now grown
all gathered 'round her soft lit tree
with families of their own.

There's whispered tree-like magic heard
in mem'ries shared and told
of loved ones now remembered,
and,
in hands that we still hold.

And when soft glows reflect and dance
in eyes you love to see,
receive, pass on all blessings found
in
Grandma's Christmas Tree.

With Love,
Grandma Janet Mary™

Mom
says,

"Every Christmas Eve when we're at Grandma's place,
there is a special feeling there, a joyous kind of grace.
And this most bles'sed kind of grace will help your heart to see
the wonder and the magic found
in Grandma's Christmas tree.

Her tree, you see, is different than a tree found in a store.
Grandma's tree is trimmed with things that mean a whole lot more,
like macaroni Christmas stars, a torn, red, tinseled bell
and glittered, colored, cardboard blocks
that spell the word Noel.

A sled made of flat wooden sticks, a tattered paper wreath,
white plastered hands that now are chipped, all dangle right beneath
the angel who sits at the top. She's made of white chiffon.
She's old but guards the tree all night
until the early dawn.

But Grandma's favorite ornament is one she did receive
from Grandpa, oh, so long ago, on their first Christmas Eve.
And each year since, high on the tree, there hangs with golden thread,
old Mrs. Claus still holding hands
with Santa faded red.

And Grandpa, he will tell you that this couple on the tree,
has come to mean your Grandma will, forever, always be,
the one and only girl for him. Your Grandpa's very sure
that Christmas magic comes from years
of loving only her."

But . . .

. . . I don't know about such things
'cause I am just a kid.
I tried to figure out her tree.
I tried. I really did.

I stared so long at all the stuff
that dangled from her tree.
I stared so long my eyes they blurred.
It was so hard to see

the magic that she talks about,
I'm not real sure it's there.
But since my Grandma tells the truth,
it must be there somewhere.

Nine older cousins
tell me,
I'm too young
to really know.
They say to understand
I'll have to wait
until I grow.

Last year I tried to fake it.

So,
I said I understood.
But they just laughed.
It made me mad.
Then Grandma said
I should . . .

". . . remember
that the tree is where
the magic
gets its start.

But
if it's to be real,
then you must feel it
in your heart."

And I remember what she said
to me last Christmas Eve.
And though I've grown an inch or two,
I still don't quite believe

or understand just what she meant.
And yet, I'm proud to say,
"I love my Grandma." That is why
I knew there was a way

to somehow find a Christmas gift
so perfect and so right,
and 'cause she means so much to me,
I thought both day and night.

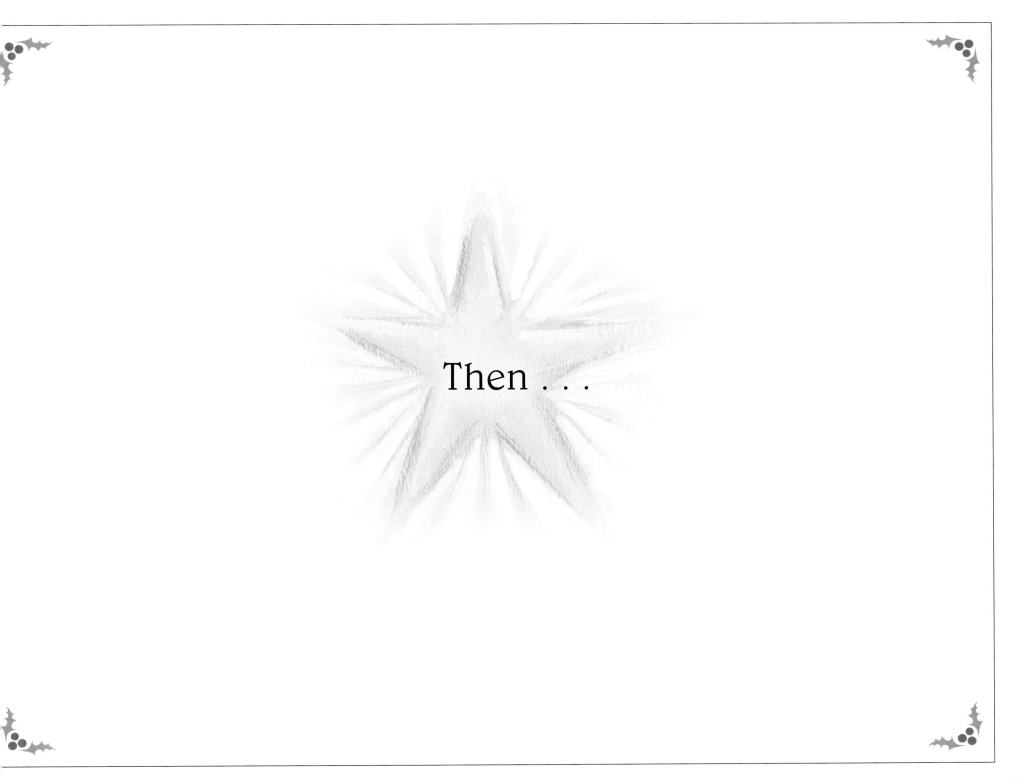

Then . . .

I got this very cool idea.

I'd make this great surprise!
Something
unbelievable
to light up her blue eyes.

For since my grandma seemed to care
about old handmade things,
and since I had no money
that could buy her diamond rings,

my genius mind thought up
thee gift,
the perfect gift from me,
a brand new, handmade ornament
to hang upon her tree.

But,
only mom and dad would know
about this gift of mine.
This secret present I would make
they said would be a sign
of how much Grandma means to me.

Yes!
I could see it now.

She'd put her hand
up to her heart.
She'd say,

"OH MY! OH WOW!"

She'd make a fuss.
She'd even cry.
She would go
on and on.

Then,
right below the angel
made of lace
and
white chiffon,

my Grandma,
she would hang my gift.
She'd hang it
on the tree.

Next to
the faded Santa
with his wife,
my gift would be.

Then, **they**
would talk among themselves,
my nine dear, older cousins.
I'd act like it was
no big deal.

But **they**
would be a buzzin',
for all of them would wish

that **they**
had thought up something cool.
But, it would be too late
and I, the smallest,
I would rule.

It was December twenty-fourth.
I made my pretzel frame.
And though I worked so carefully
somehow my gift became

a sticky, whitish, pretzeled mess.
There were these glued up clumps.
I panicked for a moment
when I saw those ugly bumps.

But, since I'm so artistic
and considered rather bright,
I smiled then glued red ribbon
to the bumps to make it right.

I next took
my school picture,

trimmed it up
so it would fit,

inside the pretzel frame
but then . . .

. . . I accidentally hit . . .

. . . my picture
to a clump of glue
that wasn't dry enough.

But, I was quick,
I used my shirt
to wipe away the stuff.

This gift of mine was coming all together
rather nice.
I took some more red ribbon,
made a bow, not once
but twice.

I glued one at the bottom,
then
I glued one at the top.
I couldn't believe the talent
oozing from my brain
NON-STOP!

Another brilliant thought,
it came!
HEY!

I'll go get the glitter!

And though I'd worked an hour now,
no way was I a quitter.
And so the glue came out again.
I put a good thick line,

around the pretzel-ribboned frame.
I saw it in my mind,
a glittered, sparkling masterpiece.
How did I get so smart?

And as I studied this rare form
of gorgeous Christmas art,
I dumped the glitter on the glue.
I used up all I had,
and when I lifted up her gift,

well....

. . . it didn't look all
that bad,
except some glitter
now was stuck
on my
school picture face,

and it would have
to stay that way
'cause it would not erase.

I looked it over
rather close
and thought,
I have the knack,

for making
Christmas ornaments.
I signed it on the back.

"To Grandma,
Merry Christmas."

Then,
I said a quiet,
"Yup!"

I got some Christmas paper,
and
I wrapped my present up.

And now at last
I stood with cousins
waiting for my turn.

Most every gift
was now exchanged.
My gut began to churn.

For Christmas Eve
was winding down,
ten presents
yet remained.

And then,
my oldest cousin spoke.
Dear Ellen
then proclaimed,

"Your grandkids thought
this year we would
do something
for your tree,

a separate gift
from each of us;
the first one is from me."

And when
my Grandma opened it,
she kissed
my cousin's cheek.

It was . . .

. . . **a store bought ornament!**

I felt my legs go weak.

I gazed
in utter disbelief
as they went in two rows

and stood before
my Grandma
with their
perfect gifts and bows.

I watched
my Grandma's face
as she accepted
with a kiss,
each angel, Santa,
Christmas bell.

**What justice
was in this?**

For each new gift
was "oohed" and "aahed"
by family sitting there.

But
in my mind,
I thought about
my glittered face
and hair.

Nine presents gone, just one was left.
I had no real way out.

I looked at Grandma who I loved,
my mind was full of doubt

and Mom and Dad they must have known.
I now felt so betrayed.

And had I known this was the plan,
somehow I would have paid

and bought an ornament like theirs
but it was way too late;

and I the youngest of them all
would now accept my fate.

My Grandma said,
"Come here, my child.
Is that gift just
for me?"

She knew it was.
But she'd be nice,
though
I knew she would see

the clumped up glue,
the glittered face.

My Grandma
wasn't blind,

and all my cousins
they would laugh
I saw them
in my mind.

The moment came. She lifted up
the pretzel-ribboned frame.
And when
she touched my face,

I knew

that no one was to blame.
I saw the tears in her blue eyes.
I didn't feel quite
so small,

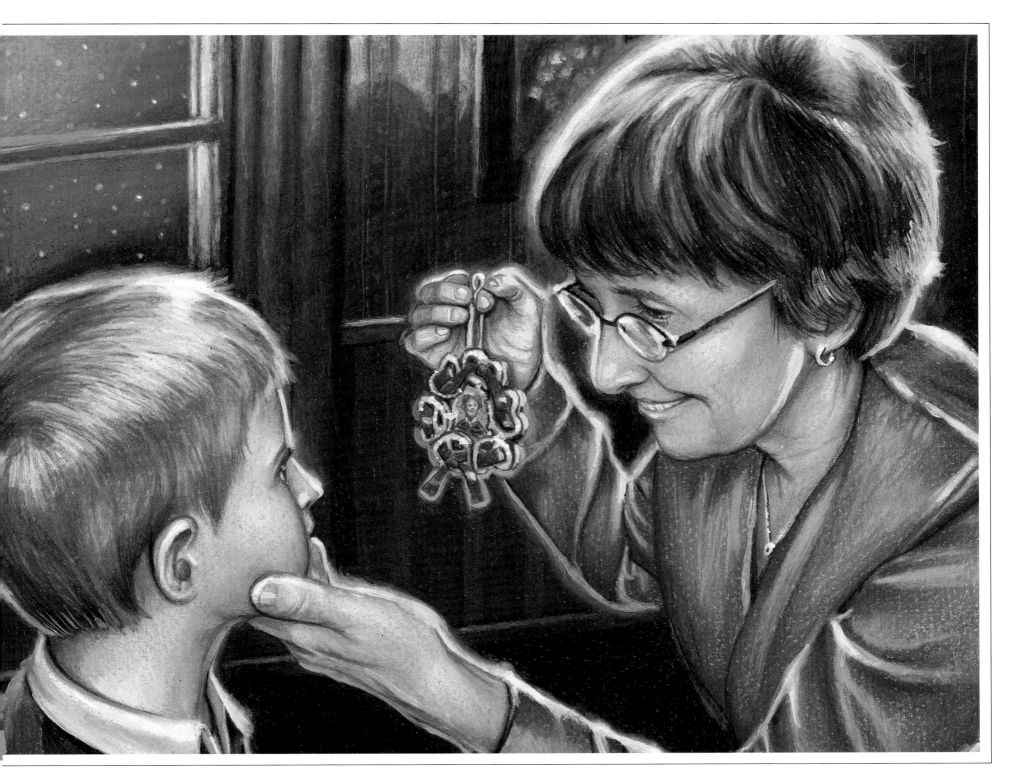

when Grandma whispered in my ear,
"I love it **most** of all."

And then she went before the tree.
She said, "Let's hang it on
this branch that sits below the angel
made of white chiffon."

And 'cause she wasn't tall enough
my Grandpa stood and said,
"Let's hang it by old Mrs. Claus
and Santa faded red."

And everyone, they clapped for me
including older cousins.
They slapped my back and rubbed my head.
Everyone was buzzin'.

And when I looked at Grandma's tree,
I couldn't hold back my smile,
'cause

**I could see the magic.
It had been there all the while.**

And now,
at last, I understood,
what Mom had said was true.

There is a special feeling here. There's mem'ries
old and new.
And I don't have to fake it now,
'cause my heart knows that we,

we all make up the magic found
in
Grandma's Christmas Tree.

How to Make a Pretzel-Ribboned Frame

Stuff You Will Need

1. small twist pretzels (about 10)
2. jar of glitter
3. red (or favorite color) of narrow ribbon
4. glue
5. scissors
6. school picture (small size)
7. small piece of white poster board
8. old scrap paper
9. pen
10. wrapping paper, scotch tape, bow, Christmas tag

Before You Start

1. Put some Christmas music on. It gets you in the right mood.
2. Get all the needed stuff listed above.
3. Think about your Grandma or the special person you are making this for.
4. Cover the table with old scrap paper, so you don't get glue and glitter on your mom's tablecloth.

How To Make It

1. Cut out an oval shape from white poster board. Make it about 4-5 inches at its widest part.
2. Good time to sign back of poster board. Address it to who you plan to give it to.
3. Take pretzels and arrange five around edge of poster board.
4. Glue five pretzels side by side onto poster board, leave half of each pretzel hanging off poster board.
5. Take other five pretzels and glue one to the top of each pretzel already positioned on poster board, making a double-decker.
6. Let glue dry for about 30 minutes.
7. Take some ribbon and cut about a 12 inch piece.
8. Very carefully, wind ribbon in and out of pretzel parts not glued to poster board.
9. Glue a string on the back of the poster board for hanging on the tree.
10. Trim up the picture and place inside opening of frame.
11. May add additional ribbon to pretzels to hide clumps of glue.
12. Make 2 bows, glue one at the top, glue one at the bottom (optional. . . that means if you want to)
13. May now put glue line on pretzels or dab here and there.
14. Sprinkle a generous amount of glitter on glue.
15. Hold up frame. Shake off any unstuck glitter. (Your mom will be so happy you put old scrap paper down.)
16. Admire your work for a few minutes.
17. Wrap very carefully and tag it.

At Christmas time, give your gift to Grandma or the special person you made this for.
Watch them go crazy over your masterpiece!